The Soccer Game

adapted by Nancy Parent
based on the teleplay by Noah Zachary,
Cole Louie, and Magnús Scheving
illustrated by Artful Doodlers

Ready-to-Read

SIMON SPOTLIGHT/NICK JR.
New York   London   Toronto   Sydney

Based on the TV series *LazyTown*™ as seen on Nick Jr.®

SIMON SPOTLIGHT
An imprint of Simon & Schuster Children's Publishing Division
1230 Avenue of the Americas, New York, New York 10020
First Edition
2 4 6 8 10 9 7 5 3 1
Library of Congress Cataloging-in-Publication Data
Parent, Nancy.
The soccer game / adapted by Nancy Parent ; illustrated by Artful Doodlers.—1st ed.
p. cm. — (Ready-to-read)
"Based on the TV series LazyTown as seen on Nick Jr."—T.p. verso.
Summary: Sportacus and his friends must figure out how to stop a soccer-playing robot run amuck.
ISBN-13: 978-1-4169-0796-1
ISBN-10: 1-4169-0796-3
[1. Robots—Fiction. 2. Soccer—Fiction.] I. Artful Doodlers. II. LazyTown (Television program)
III. Title. IV. Series.
PZ7.P2165Soc 2006
[E]—dc22
2006011772

SPORTACUS and the LazyTown kids

are playing soccer.

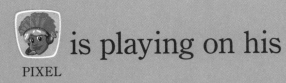 is playing on his .

PIXEL COMPUTER

"I will watch the game

from here," he says.

ROBBIE ROTTEN

wants to play too.

"How about a game?" he asks.

"Sure!" says  .

SPORTACUS

"I will play inside this 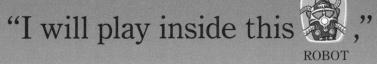,"

ROBOT

says  .

ROBBIE ROTTEN

"I will trick them!"

The game begins!

The  ROBOT trips SPORTACUS .

The ROBOT steals the BALL .

The  scores a goal.

ROBOT

"I won!" cries  .

ROBBIE ROTTEN

"I am number one!"

SPORTACUS shakes.

He is a good sport.

Then the  goes wild.
ROBOT

The  kicks!
ROBOT

The soccer  fly!
BALLS

ROBBIE ROTTEN pushes all of the BUTTONS.

Nothing stops the ROBOT!

knows what to do.

PIXEL

"To stop it," says,

PIXEL

"they must beat it!"

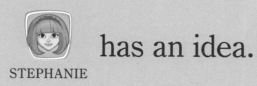 has an idea.

STEPHANIE

"If we **all** play," she says,

"we can beat it!"

and the kids

SPORTACUS

play against the .

ROBOT

The score is tied.

"Come on,  !

PIXEL

We need your help,"

says  .

STEPHANIE

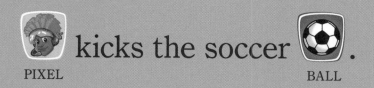 kicks the soccer .

PIXEL   BALL

He scores the winning goal!

The kids go to help the  up.
ROBOT

Is someone inside?

Surprise!

It is 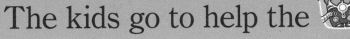 !
ROBBIE ROTTEN